I0537658

THE TALE OF

Richard Forsyth

Ross Mayhew

PROLOGUE

This is a story from 1665, and like all stories from the years that have long since passed by, it contains elements of truth, but a truth that has been coloured and layered with both myth and legend, woven in by each re-telling by each story-teller as the years and the tale echo on with the endless roll of the tide.

The version you're about to read, like all versions, centres around the most well-known, and most feared pirate of them all – Richard Forsyth, whom legend says is still sailing the seven seas this very day. In fact, the mere uttering of his name, or that of his ship "Marie's Red Revenge", with its blood-red sails, still sends shivers down the spines of all sailors and puts fear into all those who share a border with the sea. It is said a broken heart led Richard Forsyth to become the man he is today and that it was a deal with the gods has made him unable to move on from this earthly realm in which we ourselves stand today.

Like all stories, this tale has a beginning and a middle, although it somewhat lacks an end that can be confirmed as final or definitive.

So even to this day we are still left wondering just when we'll be able to finish the tale and close the book on this story and consign it to history. But it is that which makes this story feel as if it is more than mere words, more than an embellished tale, more than a simple fantasy from an age long passed, the fact it remains unfinished is what makes it feel so real and part of our lives to this very day.

CHAPTER I:
THE TALE BEGINS

W e've all looked out at sea and wondered just what lies over the seemingly endless horizons ahead of us, beyond what our eyes can behold, and it is there, over a journey of horizons and sunsets upon an island that lies just out of sight where this story began.

Richard Forsyth was born on the 19th of January 1665 to parents named Melissa and Colin who ran the island's bakery and owned the wheat fields on the outskirts of the village. While Colin was the one who would turn out the finest loaves and rolls, his flair and skill second to none and with his added personal charm making him a popular man, quick with wit but also a gentle love and care for all whom he knew; however, those with keener eyes would notice it was Melissa who was the more dominant of the pair – behind her innocent smile and carefully placed footsteps was a woman determined to be sure nothing would destroy the life she had made, protective of her husband, their business and most of all their son Richard. But not even her love could prevent what fate had in store.

The island the Forsyth family called home was small and humble; time has forgotten its name but it was said to be a month of travel over the horizon to sight any land following any direction on any wind. The village itself, a collection of cottages and shops with homes above, lay just on a single street, itself just a short walk from the quay where boats would arrive into the harbour with fish for those in the village. Looking north-west as you made port would give you a clear view down the street. You'd see the island's population going between the shops, going about their work and living a life that you could only describe as idyllic by today's terms, simple and essential. The village buildings and crop fields aside the island was mostly vegetation, full of trees, they covered and surrounded the central hill on the island with just a small clearing close to the top where the lookout shelter was located near to the summit and it was directly below that that the church lay, which itself was exactly halfway up the hill built into a nook and a path that wound down to the village.

The sun would shine brightly in the day and nights were clear and crisp as torchlight lit the town and harbour. It was a world within a world, a self-sufficient paradise located out of sight of the rest of the world where they could grow their own crops and fish the ocean surrounding them; there was a common saying of "luckier than most" amongst those that called it home. The sea that surrounded them was a crystal clear turquoise that gradually faded to a deeper blue the further from the island one sailed. This was a paradise that neither then nor now is mapped on any chart, as if it willed its way into being, ignored by those seeking to find and own all that could be found and owned.

On the tip of the horizon when looking south by south-west from the docks you would see a rock protruding from the waves – it goes by the name of Sailors Thumb and every winter mermaids would flock to the area. Stories about them would reach the island, and these were positive stories; the most common of stories was that mermaids knew the seas almost as well as the gods who made them. The world works when all lives learn to coexist and while in some areas mermaids were feared, or even hunted, around these seas they were respected and left to their own devices and no problems did arise between them and those upon the island. In fact, if you listened carefully in the depths of nights, you'd hear the mermaids singing, and often upon an evening once Colin and Melissa had put Richard to bed they'd walk the shore and listen to the soft sound of their songs rolling faintly over the waves.

The village had a Governor, Jacob Harrison, who shared his home with his wife Emily, and it is said Jacob's great-grandfather Benjamin was one of the first on the island, he and a ship full of friends responsible for laying the foundations of what others now called home. The Governor's home lay off a path to the west of the village and overlooked harbour, but despite their status neither Jacob nor Emily would stay solely in their elegant home – they'd walk or travel in horse and cart down from their home along the winding path that led south-east and taking them along the seafront. On arriving at the docks, they'd enjoy spending time with the townspeople, they would help in the church, help at the quay, like everyone else they pitched in around the village so the working day was as easy, quick and as comfortable as could be. Throughout the year parties would be hosted at their home, making use of their garden space and giving everybody a chance to relax – "a cause to celebrate for one was a cause for all to celebrate" Jacob would often say during these parties.

It was a way of life that seems impossible to imagine now. Some say the innocence is exaggerated by what would come, for the sake of added contrast, to show the difference between the light and the dark, and I suppose we can't ever be sure exactly what was, but we know what things would become and what they are today.

CHAPTER II:
THE DECADE
OF BLISS

Growing up, Richard would be educated solely by his mother – despite families being on the island it had no school, so like all mothers she would teach him the basics of reading and writing. She would make him study for four hours each morning before he was allowed to make the afternoon his own - "awake with the dawn, learn until noon and play until the rise of the moon" was her saying. As long as the children knew the important basics, most would follow in the family trade, and largely it was only the women who had a good understanding of reading and writing, so they'd make sure their children were equipped in those areas before manual labour and following a trade became their days in adolescence and adulthood.

Richard's first port of call once the learning day was done was to watch his father finish work, to tell him about what he'd learned with his mother. Richard was a keen student, a boy who would look and learn rather than talk and impose, he could learn just from watching, so he'd marvel at his father's work, noticing all the careful details, observing the whole world around him and absorbing it all. Once work was done and they were free to enjoy the late afternoon and early evening together, they'd go and walk the island, play by the sea, talk with the traders and sailors, and make the best of the day's remaining hours. Due to Melissa's protective nature, Colin would never quite give a full detailing of what he and Richard would do, they'd never seriously get in harm's way, but men young and old like to test the world and seek adventure so a few bumps and bruises wouldn't be unheard of. They would use branches as swords while playing soldiers, and they would climb trees or scale rocks to reach the highest point of the island to see if they could touch the sky, before sitting above the lookout spot just to watch the sun set into the ocean.

Richard and his father had favourite places they'd stop at, such as near the lookout as mentioned and another was a small cave that lay on the western shore of the island. It was located behind some very thick bushes and it was their own little hideaway – they'd often say to one another "we'll bury our treasure here when we're pirates". They happened upon it by chance during a game of hide and seek; Richard was climbing a tree to hide in its foliage but just a few feet up he lost his grip and fell, landing in the midst of some bushes. A little dazed and confused, he wandered further into the undergrowth and not toward the path from where he'd come, and it was there he found what would become their cave, where they would light a small fire, share a meal and talk until the sun began to fall and getting home ready for Richard's bedtime. This was their world and they embraced it fully, father and son, the best of friends.

Every evening after returning from his adventures with his father, Richard's mother would read him a story or a poem as he settled in to bed. She'd often read tales that featured mermaids, as they were her own fascination, from watching them with Colin by Sailors Thumb Rock she'd tell little stories about kings and queens and a secret world beneath the waves, but all was from her own imagination. She believed reading and telling tales of myth and legend would help her son see all the beauty the world had to offer, to encourage his own imagination. "As men know where leads to water the mermaids know where leads to land" was one of her favourite quotations.

Once the story of the evening was told, she would sing him a little song before bidding him goodnight. Her favourite song to sing was:

"Tomorrow comes as yesterday goes,
and all the time my love grows
it grows for you, my darling boy
don't let sadness dull your blue eyes
Sleep soundly tonight in your bed
as all your dreams fill your head
who knows what day they'll come true
but my darling I'll be there when they do."

She'd kiss him on the head and bid him goodnight, to sleep soundly before tomorrow's dawn.

Of course, like all boys who grow up by the sea, Richard would dream of sailing the ocean; he would even get a few lessons and be shown the basics of managing boats of various sizes from those who worked at the harbour. On land or at sea there are always stories being told of adventure, and those are the stories that will win a child's heart and mind, but he was truly happy with it being a fantasy. Tales of pirates and mermaids are exciting, but he had no thought of leaving the island – this was where he felt loved and comfortable, it was where he knew he belonged. His father would fuel his mind with adventure while his mother kept him grounded; it was a good combination, he felt free but also secure; this was his paradise, the perfect world for a growing boy approaching his tenth birthday.

CHAPTER III:
FROM BEYOND
THE HORIZON

It was ten days after Richard's tenth birthday, the 29th of January 1675 and what seemed another typical early evening. The night already long settled, the island's lookouts passing the time as always with a game of cards by candlelight, the Governor and his wife long since returned home and asleep, just like the ships resting at the docks. It was as it always was and how they thought it would forever be, another settled evening in paradise with torches lighting the town and the only sound to be heard was the gentle lapping of the waves against the shore.

Seemingly out of nowhere, as the midnight hour was close to being struck the stars that were twinkling clearly in the night sky suddenly became covered as dark clouds formed, heavy mist fell and the wind picked up and whistled through the town and around the docks, picking up both strength and speed. Those few still tending to things that needed to be done carried on attending to their duties, because even on this haven of an island of seeming forever sunshine, they would receive the occasional visit from the rain. Tonight, however, it was something far worse than heavy wind and rain that was approaching the island; some ten-to-fifteen minutes after the clouds and mist arrived, a call came from the hill above the village. The call came not from the lookout point but from the church – the vicar, The Reverend Clive Hardin, while observing the change in the weather, spotted a ship creeping from the horizon, and he shouted "flames on the water, to the south!" to those in the lookout above, and when those on the role of lookout this evening acted and inspected the sight via their looking glass, they saw the vessel and fear gripped them in an instant. It was clear from the ship's colours that this was no friendly visit; the ship itself was a charcoal black, darker than darkness and the black was raised!

Tales of pirates are always told on islands and towns that border the sea, but here they'd never come into contact with any, the island has no treasure or material to be profited from, it holds no political power. It lay either unfound or simply ignored, deemed insignificant by the respective naval fleets of the British, French, Spanish and Dutch, so what could these pirates want?

Panic gripped the island as the bell was rung. Richard was asleep in the family home but awoken by the commotion, his parents too were awoken and rushed to Richard, to protect their treasure. Even the town's own defences had no experience in such a matter as this – the island had never faced invasion, and the wait for the ship to arrive into port seemed to last an age as the winds howled. The sky grew darker than the night itself, the wind blew out all the torches that lit the street; how symbolic that would prove, the light extinguished.

The ship seemed to almost float over the waves as it approached the dock; all had run home or to a place they deemed to be safe. The moon was blocked by cloud, the only light came from the torches upon the side of the approaching vessel. The whole world fell silent, until the moment the gangplank fell, a loud thud followed by heavy footsteps. This was the moment a crew of men armed with pistols and swords came hurrying down to loot, plunder and kill. The island's team of soldiers, mostly volunteers, were dispatched of almost instantly, the fear in their eyes was obvious, they knew it was a death sentence to even attempt to stand up to these villains of the sea. The pirates wiped out the soldiers in a blink of an eye, and anyone else who was seen was killed without reason or remorse in a gruesome and wicked display of violence, the kind only a devil could comprehend or endorse.

The pirates would raid the town, going from shop to shop, home to home, taking food, money and anything else they deemed worthy; it was also a case of destruction for destruction's sake, houses set alight and livestock killed. The vicar who had first spotted their approach was captured as the church was raided; he was told his loving god is a coward and no match for the devil, and as tears ran down his face and he begged for forgiveness, he was decapitated at the altar where he would speak of the power of kindness and love.

Colin and Melissa panicked over what to do as the footsteps became louder and their fear stronger. Colin told Richard he must go to the cave and he would come find him in the morn. Melissa couldn't bear to let Richard go but Colin insisted, he knew what fate likely awaited him and his wife and couldn't bear it for his son. So, Melissa did agree with her husband and off Richard ran as fast as he could, holding a lantern taken from home and following the route suggested by his father so he'd go unseen. For all three to go would attract attention, it was a sacrifice of their safety for their son's survival.

Richard ran and made his way to the cave under the growing and deepening darkness that was consuming the island; the sounds of destruction were echoing behind him and his own footsteps, heaven was turning to hell. There was a last look back before going deep into the bushes and to the cave for safety; he saw his world burning as tears ran down his face. Once inside he headed straight for the crawl space at the back of the cave on the left-hand side – this would help keep him stay hidden from sight should the cave be found by another. Safely in the crawl space, the very spot where he and his father said they would hide their treasure, he pulled a rock in front to help cover the small opening, to hide him more so. Once hidden in the cave, Richard shut his eyes and whispered softly a song sang to him by his mother for comfort when she saw him face uncertainty or worry.

"There's a place to be, there's a place to hide,

there's a place you're safe, it is by my side

I will never hurt you, nor will I desert you

all will be well, in time, my dear."

Time passed as time does and a small amount of daylight began to enter the cave from above, the light seeping softly between the leaves that surrounded the cave and then through a gap in the rock that made the roof of the small chamber he was in. A new day was beginning, the echoes of destruction from the town had seemed to cease, so slowly but surely Richard crept out from hiding. The world seemed still but he was nervous and alone, trembling with fear and trepidation. He began to climb the hill to the spot where he and his father would watch the sun fall after an afternoon of adventure, being careful to do so without being seen and walking just off the usual pathway. When he reached the top he saw the destruction of the church, the roof destroyed by flames and the vicar's headless body which had been dragged on to the steps outside the entrance.

At the lookout station, which was now just a pile of bricks, he found a working, albeit slightly cracked spyglass. Picking it up nervously and looking through he saw so many sights that would change him and that would forever haunt his mind, the anchor of sadness had dropped and firmly locked. Firstly he saw the hanging bodies of the Governor and his wife from the balcony of their home, their blood against the mustard coloured walls facing the garden where the island's New Year celebrations were held and where many parties and moments of celebration took place all year round. He saw the bodies of those he called friends lying in the streets and the village that was his home but a skeleton of what it once was, buildings still alight, walls fallen and windows broken.

His final sight from atop the hill was a glimpse of the ship of those who had inflicted all this damage sailing away from the harbour. The vessel was cutting through the waves so smoothly and with such a gentle nature, a passage that was calm and measured, the very opposite of the horrific destruction its cannons and crew had caused.

CHAPTER IV:
AFTER THE STORM

Once the ship had gone over the horizon's edge, Richard hurried down toward the village, desperate to find his parents. As he made his way he could see some people had survived – he witnessed a few picking themselves up, lifting others and coming out of hiding now the destruction had ceased. With the winds now calm an intimidating silence gripped the island, it was in a manner so strong it seemed almost impossible to imagine that anyone would have the courage to break it.

It was in his naivety that he assumed his mother and father had also survived. He came to the bakery and without pause headed inside expecting them to greet him with arms open, but the sight he'd see upon the opening of the door was one that would cause him to pause in shock and horror. His father's body lay against the counter, his head across the room; he had been executed in the most brutal of manners. Richard couldn't summon a scream such was his anguish. He then ran for his mother, heading towards the stairs, hoping to find her reading one of her books, but it was on the stairs that he found her, lying in a puddle of her own blood from a stab wound to the stomach.

Richard ran outside, a boy so broken, a boy who'd had his world taken from him and there was no reason for it. He collapsed in a heap in the street, tired, scared and emotionally wounded. He would wake up in the home of his father's best friend, Julius Cochran, who was also employed to help tend to the wheat field on the village outskirts.

Julius could never replace Richard's father, it was a time where no words would help, all he could be was there, be someone to help Richard through the days both dark and light. In time Richard and Julius decided to carry on the work of Richard's parents by restoring the bakery and returning to work. Not much had survived, the back wall had crumbled, fire destroying the roof, but by chance Colin's navy blue jacket, which he wore as he married his bride all those years ago had survived. For a family that had little in terms of material possessions, this was very much a keepsake – "one day you'll fit into this, Richard, and your father will be proud of the man you become," said Julius; "in fact, both your mother and father will be, you'll make them proud as you walk around town in your fathers finest carrying on their good name". Richard while fighting the tears looked up to the heavens and smiled, doing them proud would be the strength to fight through these times of darkness.

So it was along with the surviving people of the village that Julius, with a young Richard by his side, would help get their world back in shape. It would be a long and difficult process both emotionally and physically, there was a lot of damage to repair, but it was either walk this road of recovery or give up and succumb to the acceptance of defeat. Julius would say to Richard when restoring the bakery and family home together that "no matter our good deeds, no matter the intent of our heart, in life we may face times of struggle, and even when we suffer the deepest of wounds and heartaches; worse than you could foresee, you must continue to press forward, to move beyond the rain, for the sun always returns in time". So together they set to their work. It was not without tears and frustrations, but it was with a resilience that not even the devil could take, it was a heaven-sent determination, because nothing goes as long as we keep hold of it, and they kept hold of their purpose.

In the weeks after a new vicar arrived, The Reverend William J. Moore, his first address at the opening of this first service was said to be as follows:

"I wish my arrival was in happier times,
darkness came and took those so
dear to so many of you here,
it came without warning, and it
came with cruel intent,
an intent to remove the light that
drives us daily, the light of love.
And now as I stand before you all I promise that
with God's love we can move beyond these times,
for the light they sought to take is never truly taken,
against the night sky those in
heaven will shine for us,

for each star is a loved one's light,
guiding us to each dawn.
I see faces both young and old before me,
times will change as the seeds of tomorrow
are planted with each day
both the old and the young on this
island will educate one another
a balance of knowledge and
discovery will be the way.
We shall never forget those who've been taken
and we shan't forget what they'd wish for us too
for them to look down and see
us triumph over sadness
and for each day to give us a smile.
I pray and I know that God will
deliver this strength to you,
we shall overcome this test and love will guide you
it will guide us all beyond the sorrow
so go forth with God by your side."

Following the service, the whole island was united in purpose, to overcome the sadness and emptiness and to return to the days of love, life and joy. It would be a long and winding road and of course Richard would walk every step required, determined to play a role in making a world as good as that as his parents had made for him. His mother would say "Love and happiness are best when shared, and they cost nothing to give", so what better way to honour her than to make sure all he did was done with those words in mind.

CHAPTER V:
THE BOY BECOMES
A MAN

The years rolled by with the tide and the village slowly recovered and grew again, new people would occasionally arrive, individuals and families of all sizes seeking to find a place where their trade would be valued. Even before the hard times fell, the island always welcomed those who could help bring a better quality of life with not only their skills and endeavour to help a community thrive, but also character and personality.

A new fort was built to help ensure better protection and it was named Harrison Fort, after Governor Harrison, partly to remember a good man but also as a reminder that the island should never again be left so vulnerable to attack. Governor Harrison was well loved and respected, but his naivety of the world's harsh realities left the island with no means of meaningful defence. Although many did say the attack that came was one to which there was no defence. But it would be that all men on the island would rotate fort duty, and all did so gladly, Richard himself of course playing his part.

One celebration the island made sure to carry on was the New Year's Eve party held at the Governor's mansion overlooking the bay. It was at one of these parties that Richard, now aged twenty-two, met Marie Gilbert, the daughter of the town's new Blacksmith. She had arrived onto the island just a few months prior and this her first time at such a celebration. Seeing her across the garden, he was willing to give her his heart in that instant – he hadn't given thought to dating much in his young life, such was the need to grow up fast, to help and support the village and its people in becoming prosperous in both business and spirit. However, even a man so focused in his duties cannot defeat the instinct and desire he felt upon seeing Marie – it was an attraction like no other – before words were even exchanged.

He steeled his courage, fighting back the nerves as he walked across the grass with footsteps so gentle not even a passing snail need even fear the tread of his boot. "Good evening," he said softly. "Forgive me but I saw you from across the garden, and would like to introduce myself. My name is Richard, Richard Forsyth. You are new to the town, are you not, miss?"

"Good evening, sir, yes I am, my name is Marie, Marie Gilbert, I moved here with my father to settle somewhere new following the death of my mother, to help us find peace and renewed purpose."

"I am so sorry to hear this, I, too, am without a mother, or indeed a father, so I can empathise with your pain, but I hope this new venture brings you happiness in your future, despite the scars of your past."

Marie smiled and thanked Richard for his kind words; they would go on to share stories, stories from their own childhoods and their dreams.

Under crisp moonlight in the first hours of a new year they shared a dance together as the band played a final selection of songs. There was an instant connection, a natural rapport and comfort between Richard and Marie. They'd continue talking once the party was coming to an end, now approaching three o'clock in the morning. They parted with a simple goodbye when Marie's father took her and himself home. There was a lingering look as they did part that suggested this was more than just the beginning of a new friendship.

The morning after the night before and the new year got underway as any other of recent times. Richard was now single-handedly running the bakery, which naturally took a large portion of his day. Early to rise a way of life but he would still have the late afternoons and onwards to himself. Julius continued to take care of the wheat supply – it kept him busy, but he was a man who liked to be busy, even when now approaching his sixtieth year. As when a boy, when the late afternoon would arrive Richard would go for a walk in the village, of course now without his father's company; he would instead pass time sharing moments with friends. His first port of call was to the village's public house, named "The Anchor Inn" but he never liked to stay there too long, because as the afternoon went on to become the evening and the drinks were consumed, more of the stories of what happened before, the attacks on the town would be told, and hearing those tales he could never bear, so he'd soon be off to meet Marie so they could spend time together and take in the evening air.

Marie's days were quite different to Richard's – she'd spend them with her father Dennis who would work all day in his workshop, from sun up to sun down, plying his trade as a blacksmith, making whatever may be needed. Marie would help keep father company, bringing him refreshments and tending to their home while he earned a wage. She'd often play games with the children who passed by; she was much loved by everyone but come the evening her time was her own and as her father settled down to relax with a book, she'd be on her way to meet Richard.

When alongside Marie, Richard felt an ease he'd never known before, and together they'd walk the shore. Richard would show her the places that meant so much to him from times with his parents, including the cave where he and his father would hide and pretend to bury their treasure. Marie was amazed by how a man who'd known so much grief could still be so loving, gentle and optimistic, while he was equally enamoured of her ability to move into a new world with such ease following her own hardships. She seemed to take on everything with such ease, the loss of her mother, the moving to a new town; there was a strength to her, he felt safe and loved just in her presence, just as she did with him.

It was atop the hill close to the rebuilt lookout station they shared their first kiss, the stars had just begun to shine when Richard leaned in to kiss her. The stars shone in her eyes and their lips met, they then lay together until the small hours, together in a blissful silence settled into each other's arms. Richard cut it fine for work the next morning after seeing Marie home, but he had a smile on his face and in his soul, the kind he hadn't experienced in many a year.

More dates came and went, they were simple, walks and meals shared, sometimes even just sitting and watching the waves together, seeing them gently move against the shore and it was there, just seven weeks from their first date, Richard was down on one knee asking for Marie's hand in marriage. As soon as he dropped to his knee the joyful tears began to fall from her eyes and a "Yes" came, almost before he had even finished asking for her hand in marriage.

Upon getting up from bended knee they embraced, and soon plans were underway for their wedding, with everyone keen to help where they could.

There wasn't much in the way of waiting – the wedding took place toward the end of the month on Melissa's twenty-first birthday, the 22nd of March. Richard was in his father's navy jacket while Marie in traditional white dress and was given away by her widowed father Dennis. A wedding in the village was a rare occasion, the service simple and the church packed to witness the exchange of their vows. Of course, once the service was complete this meant another party with games, dancing and drinking going on deep into the night. Richard and Marie snuck away early as neither were particularly keen on fuss, so they bid goodnight to Dennis and Julius and went out beyond the party lights. It was all they wanted was to be married and now they were, so they left their own wedding party for their first night together as man and wife.

There was no honeymoon to be had and now that they were married they lived together as man and wife above the bakery, as had Richard's parents before him. They had all they needed in the world, they had each other, there was no need or desire for more. For the good times and bad they were together forever, two souls who had found their home next to one another.

The turning of the tide had given Richard reason to smile.

CHAPTER VI: THE BLACK WINDS RETURN

It had taken many years and a lot of hard work, but the village was smiling again. The attacks in 1675 would never be forgotten, and lying just before the narrow pathway which led up to the church a small garden was created, and in it a memorial to all those who had lost their lives following the attacks. The garden had a central flowerbed with a path that lay around its circumference, and it was equipped with seating areas for people to come so they could remember and reflect. A sign at the memorial garden's entrance read "Those who've passed are the lights that shine long after the sun falls, we shan't forget them for their light shall not fade". Richard would often stop by here and think of his parents. At first anger would fill his heart, but now it was smiles of the fond memories, the realisation he was carrying on their legacy and name, he knew they'd be proud of him and the life he'd made. He would go to their graves once a week and tell them details about his life, such as his courtship and marriage to Marie and the latest news, that Marie was now carrying his child.

As he sat on the bench before returning home to Marie, another slowly descending evening sun became masked by the sudden arrival of dark clouds, pushed to the island by the howling black winds of death. The whistle of the winds made it sound as if ghosts lay down every lane and turn. Richard's heart dropped, his stomach felt uneasy; he knew what was to come. Panic engulfed the island, Marie came looking for Richard, knowing he was spending time at the memorial gardens. He ordered her to go home, telling her it was just a storm and she shouldn't worry herself so needlessly. The chaos all around her told her he was lying, it was clear, even if to try and protect her and even though she was desperately wanting to believe his performance of calm, his eyes spoke the truth and showed the fear of what was to come.

In that moment they heard a voice call from the lookout "Sails!! They've returned!!". They could do nothing but watch as the ship approached, again it silently glided through the sea and this time Richard wasn't made to hide, he was stood by the fountain in the village centre where he'd met Marie as he journeyed to her and her to him. Together they watched the scene unfold as the pirates made their way from the harbour to the village, seeing them strike down anyone who dared even look at them, let alone challenge them.

"What do they want?" asked Marie.

"I don't know, my angel," he replied. "I did not know then and not since have I learned what they seek, it seems their only motive is to cause pain."

Marie began to become more and more frightened by the panic around her, the air felt cold and escape impossible.

"Head to my safe place!" Richard implored. "You will survive this if you go now, and I will come find you once calm is restored," he told her.

At that moment of telling Marie to find safety, Richard spied the ship's Captain standing on deck, watching his men rush to the town to cause destruction as they did twelve years ago. He was stood motionless, a tall man, with long ginger beard and seemed to not react to any of the terrors going on in front of his eyes, a calmness only a devil could hold in such moments surely? There was a split second, however, of eye-contact between the pair – this was the man who had ordered the attack that saw his parents murdered, and Richard, who was otherwise calm and good natured, felt an anger he'd not felt before.

His weapon drawn, Richard went to do his part in at least stave off this latest attack, ordering Marie to flee to safety, but it was in that very same moment he was concussed by some falling timber following the cannons taking out a nearby building, blood coming out of the wound as he lay motionless. His last sight was rushing footsteps and the last sound was that of Marie screaming before he lost consciousness.

The following morning Richard awoke. The village was again quiet, but with flames and broken homes all around him, and of course many dead in the street. In a haze he eventually stood up, blood on his body and clothes; he was weak and weary and as tried he to focus onto the shore he saw no glimpse of the demon ship sailing away this time; they'd long since gone and their destruction long since done.

A look behind him brought him straight back to his knees, his wife Marie lay motionless, blood all around her body. He crawled toward her, shouting and begging for her to be okay, but he knew she wasn't, she was dead along with many, many others, more so than before; it didn't look as if the island could recover from this a second time. For one final time Richard held Marie close, tears streaming down his face as he whispered to her "Farewell, my angel bride" before setting her down gently.

They say it was that moment where he changed, his face became stern, anger consumed him; he had now lost his mother, his father, his wife and best-friend and their unborn child. This was a man who had recovered so well and played such a role in helping to restore the town, even as a young boy, but now there was no way back for Richard. Approached by a family friend inquiring if he was okay, Richard just paused for half a second and gave a dead-eyed stare, then spoke in a manner which held no warmth, saying "Lay Marie to rest so God can find her, and pray that in time hopefully I may find him too and be with her again, but from this moment I must now see that a debt that cannot be paid in gold is collected" – and then in an eerily calm manner, he picked up his sword, walked toward the docks, found himself a row boat and set out to sea.

He had seen the man who was responsible for so much pain and felt it was time the devil felt the fire, and that he was the one to make sure it happened. He had no plans, but knew what he must now dedicate his life toward from this moment on: revenge!

CHAPTER VII: A FRIENDSHIP FORMED IN HEARTACHE

I n a boat taken from the harbour and nothing on him but the clothes he was in and a sword pulled from a corpse by the dockside, Richard was on his way, but to where was yet unknown. The waves grew rougher with each fathom he rowed and as the island that had forever been his home fell behind horizon.

He was lost at sea for days, ravaged with hunger and thirst but holding no regrets. It was on the evening of his fourth full day at sea that he spotted a shoreline and so with the remains of his weakening strength he did all he could to get himself there.

Strong winds made the sea rough to navigate, but he just about managed to get to the beach; however, no sooner had he left his vessel did he collapse on the sand with the waves lapping against him.

He awoke sometime later, finding himself on a pile of straw, bleary eyed and looking around his new surroundings. His attention was caught immediately by that of a figure across the room drinking from a mug with an empty plate beside him. Hearing Richard move as he woke, the figure spoke: "You ought to be careful arriving on the sands like that, this isn't a welcoming town, you have to earn your place."

Richard in a haze spoke sharply back. "I seek not to be welcomed, I am seeking revenge. Who are you? Why am I here?"

"My name is Ed, Edward McVeigh, you're in Champoton, welcome to Mexico, now come on over here and get yourself a bite to eat."

Richard dragged himself up, and noticing his sword was missing he gave Ed a look of concern, wondering if he could trust this man. Ed simply said, "Your blade is safe, now come and get some food, tell me your tale." So over some food Richard shared his story. Ed said it sounded like the man who attacked his village was Captain Firebeard. "He's been roaming the seas for near 15 years now, they say he kills because the screams of his victims drown out the screams the devil placed in his own head as he bargained for his freedom."

Richard probed: "So he seeks nothing but to kill?"

"That's right, so best stay away from the sea, stay on land and move forward," said Ed.

Richard just grinned to himself and then spoke. "One more question: why the name Captain Firebeard?"

"He's a man whose true name remains unknown, but those who have survived his attacks tell tale of his ginger beard but also his love of making sure a town is all but burned to the ground during his raids."

Richard knew this only too well from first-hand experience, so he offered no further question and instead asked Ed to share his own tale.

Ed told the story of how he was once first mate to his best friend, his own brother named John McVeigh. Together raised in Scotland from an early age, himself barely twenty years old as they took to life at sea, they ran an honest trade in tea and spices until the day they heard the tale of a fallen ship that held unclaimed gold in quantities beyond imagination. It was said to be located on the North shore of South America, laying wrecked in a bay dubbed "Devil's Mouth", named so as two tall rocks stood either side of the entrance to the bay, which locals claimed to be the horns of Satan. No ships are said to ever have sailed out again once in, other tales say the devil himself stands guard and the cost of escape was one that which no man would pay. Ed wanted no part in this mission which he deemed foolish; his brother, however, was determined and in a furious row cast overboard all who disagreed, even his own brother and first mate. It was the last he ever saw him, two brothers once bound together so tightly suddenly torn apart by the lure of gold. Ed found himself washed up on a beach in Mexico as his brother John ventured further south in search of the gold from Devil's Mouth.

"Have you not tried seeking him?" inquired Richard.

Ed replied, "That was quite some time ago, he'll have met his fate by now. I've had to start again and learn a new life; in time you will too, don't let the quest for revenge drive you, my friend."

Richard paused for a second, grinned to himself once more and steadily said, "We must all pay for the heartache we cause, and I'd say god, or perhaps the devil isn't doing enough to make sure costs are paid." He then carried on eating, finishing off his meal and the two men got to know each other some more. They'd been talking all evening long under the glow of the lanterns in Ed's humble home, but it was daylight before they realised, so Ed had to set to work at the docks while Richard rested some more after his ordeal. "Don't be getting used to it always being this easy," quipped Ed as he shut the door and left Richard to rest.

It was later that evening that Ed showed Richard the town of Champoton, showing him where he worked on the dock. Ed's primary job was to help keep the ships maintained, to help fix any repairs that may need attending to upon their docking at the harbour. It was later at his favourite bar, that they shared drinks and yet more stories, stories about mermaids, pirates and myths of the sea, and one such story was that of the Isle of Manana Eterna, where it's said lies the way to travel a million horizons without ageing. Although no sailor alive has ever seen the Island, so where the story came from it isn't certain, but the notion of never ageing appealed to Richard as he knew not how long his own quest would take to complete.

The fascination of the story aside, Richard's determination for revenge and the anger within were still very much present and this would lead to something of more than a mild commotion in the pub where they drank. Feeling the effect of the rum they'd been steadily consuming over several hours, and in getting up from his seat to visit the bar for another round, Richard stumbled and fell into a local man. It was before even a word could be exchanged the trouble began – there was a quick glance in the eye and Richard didn't take it to be friendly, so without even a thought he pulled his sword and slashed the man's stomach in one move! Bedlam broke out, Richard the target, but it was a case of all against all, frustrated men releasing their pent up rage, glasses were broken, stools thrown, windows smashed and a fire soon raging after one local drunk fell into the fireplace, it quickly spread.

Ed was stunned; he knew he wouldn't last long in this town after this – people see who welcomes another, and if they don't fit, the blame is on them. It had taken Ed years to become accepted in the town, keeping his head down and working hard at the harbour, but he had just brought in a man who has not only killed but destroyed a very popular watering hole, the latter causing the most upset in these parts. Both men fled amongst the chaos. Ed stood looking at the burning pub from the beach, as he hid from those seeking him out; he then heard Richard shout, "So, Ed, shall we go and find forever?" He was stood by a dinghy. Ed ran toward him. "I suppose I have little choice – it's either death here or take my chances at sea, looks like I'm a sailor again."

Together against the light of the burning pub they set out along the coast. There was no time for Ed to return home; both men knew it was now or never. They had on them only the clothes on their backs and the swords at their belts. Richard, a man once so steady, so gentle and so reliable had, in 48 hours, met a man, destroyed his world and taken him to stand alongside in a quest of a sailor's myth, to find the Isle of Manana Eterna to ensure that revenge could be taken against the man who darkened his eyes of once a blue so bright.

CHAPTER IIX:
THIEVES OF THE SEA

Richard and Ed were now companions, and for better or worse, these two men who'd only known one another a matter of sunsets had to now set their sights on procuring a vessel that would be efficient enough in carrying them over all the seas and in all conditions, as they hunted both the Isle of Manana Eterna and Captain Firebeard. At Ed's recommendation it was in Progreso, just a bit further along the coast of Mexico, that they felt they could obtain a suitable vessel. So they waited, and with good fortune their wait was brief, which considering their lack of food was most welcomed. A ship that had not long pulled into port lay at the docks, a sloop named "Buscador de Mar". The current crew on board seemed thin but also enough to sail as the cargo was being unloaded and men went seeking rest and pleasure after their recent voyage.

Together they boarded the ship, through stealth at first, ducking and weaving behind any objects they could to get as close as possible, in shallow waters under the docks, before beginning to scale the stern. Once on board, sheer force and courage was the only attitude that would be successful – you couldn't wander on to a ship in such a manner and survive without showing your intent with purpose and passion, with a rage that would send demons cowering. Richard had this fire within him burning as soon as his boots hit the deck, his indifference to life saw him cast his blade toward anyone who stood even close by; he and Ed acted and attacked early, when the ship was at its emptiest. Crewmen were pushed into the sea, the gangplank was removed before anyone knew what was taking place, and the first man to challenge them on deck met with a death so barbaric it shook all the others into submission. Stories of pirates are told to bring fear, but to see these acts first-hand induces a fear that cannot be expressed without tears. The name of the man who challenged Richard is lost to history, but his corpse was forever on the mast from that day, pinned by his own sword via his neck to the wood beneath the main sail, and Richard laid out his terms no sooner than a second after the body was pinned, blood dripped and the challenger tried to scream as his final breaths were being drawn.

"I seek revenge, but I do not wish to harm you or your friends." These words were spoken calmly by Richard as his sword dripped with the blood of the recently murdered crewman who had dared to challenge him. "You can join me and you'll earn more than you could have imagined via honest toil, and those who aren't man enough must leave now or face the fate to which this man's foolish bravery led him!" There was a cold silence; even Ed, who was stood directly behind Richard, looked on with an eye of concern given the events he had just witnessed and unwittingly helped take place. He knew only too well of Richard's passion for revenge, but didn't believe so soon on their journey would he see the lengths he would take to ensure it.

The Captain of the "Buscador de Mar" simply offered up his role; he was a weak man, clearly chosen for the role for his skills as a sailor, not as a fighter. The fact that he did nothing, not even speak, as his crewman was so barbarically killed by Richard is perhaps why his crew offered no fight – why defend the ship of a man who would not defend them? Perhaps they'd been sailing the easy and calm waters for too long? He met his end by his own crew at Richard's demand: "End his captaincy and take on mine, or know the price you'll pay."

As the screams of terror came from the captain of old, Richard made his way to the captain's cabin, now his. Richard and his first-mate Ed spoke of their plans. Richard knew that he was no master of the sword, he knew surprise and theatre had led to their victory today; so behind closed doors he instructed Ed to help him and to find towns where he could improve his fighting skills but also locate the riches he promised his new crew. Ed set about helping, pointing out the towns and ports he felt could be likely ports where they'd achieve such success; by hook or by crook he had to stay on Richard's side. Ed was now sailing the dark tides – was this the price of kindness to a stranger, or was this always his fate, to become a pirate?

In a matter of months they rode the waves of destruction, terrifying all whom they encountered, ships were sunk, gold was claimed and experience gained. While always looking for clues to where Captain Firebeard might be, or may have been of late, but he was a very difficult man to find. It's said his ship always appears from dark clouds on the sea and has never been traced once it leaves the sight of its latest attack.

The battles they fought weren't always easy as Richard learned his trade and mastered the blade; he suffered cuts, scars and even the loss of his right hand during one battle off the coast of Cuba. Ed always watched his back though, knew when to step in and knew when to hang back. Together they were doing well, better than could have ever been imagined when they left Champoton; they never went hungry, money not an issue and they had built a good, strong and loyal crew to lead to battle, even if the ultimate battle seemed to be never arriving.

Over the years it had come to pass that Captain Firebeard's name wasn't the only name people feared, but also the name of Richard Forsyth and his ship which he christened "Marie's Red Revenge"; with its red sails, painted in the blood of his victims, it would bring terror to the hearts and minds of all who sighted her at sea.

CHAPTER IX: SOME VALUE REMAINS

Richard's value for life had been fast diminishing since the day he lost Marie, he had taken countless lives, both personally and via the attacks his crew carried out in his name. From the day he began his mission for revenge against Captain Firebeard, his soul grew darker with each passing hour.

He wasn't a man completely without soul, however, although rumours did say he was born without one as his legend grew; "the angels forgot him" was the saying. It was upon one crossing of the ocean and approaching the coast, he happened to catch glimpse of another ship that had men in longboats casting their nets, blades and aiming their pistols and spears to the waves, as if they were perhaps some trying to make a kill for some food, "perhaps a whale, or a shark?" he thought, but it looked suspicious and not a practice Richard had ever seen before. Marie's Red Revenge crept ever closer and saw that this was no mere case of starving men trying to survive; this was a mermaid hunt. Richard had heard of these but never seen one with his own eyes. It lit a fire deep within him due to the way his mother spoke highly of these creatures of the seas.

Growing up, his mother would tell him stories of mermaids and their importance in the sea, how they would rid the world of the selfish men by luring them to their deaths, and thus only men of pure intent would survive. Richard and his crew were quickly drawn to action, sinking the ship with cannon fire as it lay anchored off the coast and leaving the men with no place to run once the man-on-man combat had begun.

It was all over in a flash; many of those hunting the mermaids fled once they saw the blood red colour of the sails of Marie's Red Revenge. Those who survived went running into the woods that lay just off the beach, their screams still heard as they went out of sight of those on the beach and in the bay. A small group of mermaids, four to be exact, swam out to sea, beyond the burning wreckage of their attackers' ship, which was taken down by the cannons of Marie's Red Revenge. While those four mermaids swam to safety, however, one did remain in the bay. Richard himself walked up toward them, he was up to his chest in the crystal blue sea that had been turned red by the battle. This sole mermaid was next to the body of a merman, holding his lifeless corpse. Richard spoke: "We were not quick enough with our action, I am deeply sorry, who was he to you?"

The mermaid replied tearfully, "My husband, my King, I am his Queen, Queen Gabrielle, and now I must look after my people without him, how am I to do this?" She said this while slowly raising her gaze to meet that of Richard's.

"You will find a way because you need to," he said. It was a rare moment where he felt another's suffering; it was clear he didn't want her to carry the weight of sadness that had been given to him by Captain Firebeard.

Her fallen husband, King Derroll, was laid to rest. Richard and his crew attended from above the waves, the service itself taking place beneath them in the depths of the ocean. Queen Gabrielle was grateful for Richard's intervention and for saving those he could, even if not her husband – she knew that to find a human who cared for mermaids was rare. This was the formation of an everlasting alliance between him, his crew and the mermaids, which was made more secure by the knowledge that Richard came from the island where there was such respect for the mermaids. Richard would tell Queen Gabrielle of those days, and the stories his mother had told him.

That evening while sat on deck, as the sun dipped over the horizon, Richard heard Gabrielle call his name, so he got in a longboat and dropped to the waves to talk with more ease beside her. She said she'd been speaking to his first-mate Ed and about their quest to find and take revenge upon Captain Firebeard. "I do not know where he lies, I am sorry to say, but I am informed you seek the Isle of Manana Eterna, is that correct?" she asked.

"That is true. Do you know where to find it?" Richard responded, barely leaving a pause between her words and his own.

"Yes, I do, but it is an island that the Gods only allow to be seen once a year – once visited it fades until a cycle of the sun is complete," she explained. "My husband possessed the map that will lead the way, but I can only take you and you alone; your crew must wait here above our home until you return. Is this satisfactory?" she enquired.

"Yes, take me there, please," Richard again hurriedly responded. The agreement was in place: Gabrielle would take Richard to what he did seek, setting out as the full moon hangs in the sky the following evening. Another bit of information she did share – "to gain access to forever one must trade a part of their heart, to sacrifice that which is dearest to obtain time." Richard wasn't concerned with that piece of information at that point, he just wanted to be sure to reach the island to increase his chances of revenge.

Seeing the excitement in his eyes she spoke but once more, to be sure he knew the reality and not the dream. "The island will also tempt you with safety, but you must remove yourself from that lure to obtain what you desire." It felt like yet more riddles from Queen Gabrielle before she did bid Richard

"Goodnight" and swam to the depths. He paused for a mere second or two to think on the words she spoke but it's clear he was fuelled by the chance of getting his hands on time, and thus also a step closer to the revenge he craved.

CHAPTER X:
THE WALKING
DEAD MAN

True to her word, Queen Gabrielle met Richard as the moon shone bright and together they navigated the sea throughout the night, Gabrielle swimming and Richard rowing his boat following her path. The sky was clearer than it had ever been, shooting stars seemed to dance and the sea was eerily calm, everything around him seemed to reflect and glimmer, even in the darkness. The only ripples on the waves were those from his oars as he moved over the reflection of the moon and stars; from afar it would seem like two skies mirrored.

No words were spoken during the voyage and Richard's compass would erratically shift. There was no way to mark or map this journey; he had to trust the path he was being led along.

The sun began to rise, and out of the morning mist that lay on the sea an island appeared. Richard rode to the shore and got out; Gabrielle got out of the sea and stood beside him. "It's here I must leave you, I know where this path leads you and it's not one I can share," she said. He turned toward her and she gave him a kiss on the cheek; it was the first time he had felt warmth since he set out on this journey of revenge so many years ago. Gabrielle spoke once more, whispering softly to him: "When the sun falls so we must cast our wish, and to sail to the end we must ask Lir to take us to the edge," and placed in his hand a coin, and before he could even think of a word to say in return she dived back into the ocean. He watched her swim out of sight, keeping his eyes on her to the last.

Richard was now stood alone, on an island that, if myth were to be believed, held the key to immortality. He also knew not the way back home, but that was his second concern; the first was to explore the island and locate what he had come for, more time, because he had seen first-hand just how short life could be and he couldn't let time take him from his quest to end the terror Captain Firebeard had placed in so many.

The island was small and circular, the beach was like a ring around the trees, which themselves were like a ring surrounding the rock in the centre that protruded above the treetops by at least 10 feet into the air. The only direction that seemed a viable option was a pathway that lay straight ahead and went into the trees that concealed the rocks behind them. A short battle through some branches led Richard straight into a cave that seemed to resemble the very cave where as a boy he had hidden from Captain Firebeard's first attack on his village, on the island he once called home. He found a comfort in being there, a tear even fell from his eye; he found himself sitting there, embracing the familiar, singing the songs of childhood and all the happy memories returning. It was not long until he fell into a sleep, the comfort of the familiar eased his soul to a point of rest he'd been unable to reach since losing Marie.

It was upon waking from his sleep that he remembered and sought after the small crawl space to the left of the entrance where he would lay concealed from sight during the attacks of 1675, and also where he and his father would speak of burying their treasure when they became pirates. This area was now filled with water, but Richard did see a soft light that was twinkling from beneath the surface as he inspected further. Owing to no other option, he decided to go into the water and follow the light. He swam through a very narrow passage and came out to a catacomb where lay a chest, just casually resting upon a large singular rock in the middle of this pool of water in which he had surfaced. Sunlight was creeping in from a hole above and falling down right upon the chest. There was no mistaking this was the prize he had been seeking, with a light upon it like he was guided to it by a power not of this earth. He believed it to be the guidance of Marie, helping him to avenge her killing.

The chest looked spotless, as if it had just been freshly laid there. Upon its lid was a bronze plaque with the words "Love is treasure, time costs love" inscribed. Richard tried to prise it open with his sword and breaking the solid silver lock, but it couldn't be done, no matter how much force was applied. Then he looked closer at the lock; the hole was not shaped for a key, at least not a key Richard had seen before, it was just a circle and nothing more. As the light from above faded Richard recalled the sacrifice spoken of by Gabrielle and read once again the words on the chest. It was in this moment he removed his wedding ring, the one thing still connecting him to Marie and his former self, and placed it into the circular lock. There was a gentle click as the ring was pushed firmly in place, deep where there was no way to grab purchase to remove it now it had been placed; the lid could, however, now be lifted.

Inside a clear bottle and a note, the note simply read "Drink me and become the living dead". Richard paused for just a moment – even a man so hell-bent on revenge knew if any point was the one he could not turn back from this was it. He had felt comfort and warmth from Gabrielle, a reward that no doubt came from his decision to defend another and not to just attack, kill and steal, which had been his life since he left home. But the memories of home and all he had lost were still too powerful, and brought more to life by being on the Isle of Manana Eterna, his memory of Captain Firebeard sailing away unmoved by the pain he had caused relit the fire of revenge and in that moment of pure anger he opened the bottle and necked its contents.

A rumble came, lightning struck through the hole above where previously the light had danced its way in, the bolt going straight through Richard. His eyes they say changed then, already darkened due to his loss and suffering, now they were darkened and soulless, as if they held all the sadness in his heart; never again could light find a way into his soul.

He walked with calm purpose back to his boat and set out to sea. It seemed within only a matter of minutes he was back at his ship, back on board Marie's Red Revenge and reunited with his Ed and his men. Ed noticed the change, not just from Richard's much darkened eyes, but there was a different feeling and force emanating from Richard, there was another force now driving him, not just the lust for revenge.

Richard and his crew would immediately return to their murderous ways, striking wherever they made port, taking gold when they had no need to, and ending lives that had so much to give. His legend was growing; no longer was he known as Richard Forsyth but instead Richard Forsyth was "The Walking Dead Man".

CHAPTER XI:
ON THE SEAS
OF REVENGE

The Walking Dead Man sailed the seven seas for seven years, causing untold pain and destruction. He and his crew killed many men, stole countless gold, but for all held in their hold, no coin was more important to Richard than the coin given to him by Queen Gabrielle all those years ago. He kept it in the inside chest pocket of his father's blue coat, which he had worn since he had become a man.

Richard was a man now caught in an ageless spell, but his crew were not. His first mate Ed while long resigned to this lifestyle and enjoying its rewards of women and gold, he was fast growing tired of the chase; he wasn't a young man even when they had met and while his experience was valuable at sea and in battle, he couldn't do this forever.

"How haven't we found him!!" Richard screamed. "I've searched every sea, every port, and yet, and yet, no matter how soon we hear news of his ship there is no sign of him, or it upon our arrival – where does he go?!" The frustration was overwhelming, and with plenty of riches the crew didn't have the same determination to carry on their pursuit as they once did; it was only the fear of their Captain that kept them attached to the mission. There had been moments when in frustration he had killed his own crew for showing weakness or a lack of willing in front of him.

It was early evening, the sun still in the sky and the ship at a point in the ocean where no matter the direction sailed, land was weeks away. Richard was deep in a dream, a dream where he recalled the words spoken to him by Queen Gabrielle, "and to sail to the end we must ask Lir to take us to the edge". He awoke suddenly, the air was still, not even a breeze could be felt and the ship quiet as could be. He crept from his cabin and toward the front of the boat, looking longingly out ahead. He then put his hand into his jacket pocket and pulled out the coin he was given the day he became The Walking Dead Man.

The coin's markings were a whirlpool on one side and what looked to be a gate on the other; around the gate were the words, which when translated from the language spoken by the mermaids, read: "gates open when we look beyond them with purpose".

In this moment of clarity as the sun began to fall into the sea that Richard realised what Gabrielle had given him the coin and whispered words for; he flicked the coin into the sea and screamed to the heavens "Lir, take me to the edge". It was said that such was the passion in his voice that he woke the Gods, thunder came in an instant, on what was prior a day where not even a whisper of a cloud was seen. A wall of water arose in a sudden gust around the ship, and a whirlpool formed within; the crew were thrown about as the pace accelerated, crew men securing themselves to Marie's Red Revenge by any means they could to avoid being thrown into the ocean.

To avoid losing his balance, Richard drew his blade and drove it with force into the deck and held on tightly while singing a song his mother would sing to him as a young boy – "tomorrow comes as yesterday goes, and with all passing time my love grows". The song gave him comfort in moments of uncertainty, and this was such a moment. The pace kept quickening as water spun beneath and around them, while thunder and lightning danced above. It seemed to go on for an age and leaving the ship now was impossible for any crew man as the water around the ship was spinning so fast that it kept all on board, but yet still they held on where possible for safety, unsure of not only what was happening but what was to come.

Suddenly the pace began to slow, the wall of water gently fell away and the rumble of thunder eased to silence. At first much seemed the same, just ocean for miles and miles, and the sun began to rise ahead of them. Just a moment later as they readjusted to what they deemed normality, a rushing sound soon caught the crew's ear as Richard returned his blade to his belt. The sea was falling in around them, and before they knew it just a few metres away seemingly bottomless waterfalls lay off the Port, Starboard and Stern of the ship, the only direction to go was forward.

As the sun reached the top of the sky the call came from the lookout of a ship ahead. Richard took out his spyglass and the second he saw the ship with his own eyes a huge smile broke out upon his face: it was the unmistakable ship of Captain Firebeard, "The Silent Reaper" lay dead ahead. Marie's Red Revenge approached with purpose, the narrow path that guided them soon fell away behind and they found themselves in a cylinder of sea, a ring in which to do battle. There was no escape, rushing waterfalls that seemed to fall forever lay around the edge but this didn't put fear into Richard – The Walking Dead Man had wanted this battle for what seemed a lifetime and the moment was finally here.

CHAPTER XII:
TWO DEVILS MEET

The Silent Reaper and Marie's Red Revenge were floating board and board, cannon to cannon. A silence louder than any storm deafened the sea for just a few seconds, although the seconds felt more like hours, the way time slows when one looks at the ocean or a loved one. Then in the blink of an eye, fighting broke out, cannons fired, swords and pistols drawn, both ships invaded by each other's crew. For a short time, Richard and Captain Firebeard stood on their respective ships at the wheel, just looking at one another as chaos ensued around them, their cold stares almost daring, taunting the other to make the first move. The waves that were once calm, soon began to rise higher and the black wind of death began to howl.

Richard was to be the first of the two captains to make a move, stepping on to The Silent Reaper and battling his way to where his enemy stood. As he made the way across the deck, taking out anyone who blocked his path, be it the crew of his enemy or those from his own ship. It was while removing his sword from the stomach of another that he showed the true lengths he would go take to reach Captain Firebeard. He saw his first-mate Ed make an approach toward Firebeard, and without hesitation Richard pulled out his pistol and fired, sending Ed to the deck hard, blood pouring from the wound to his shoulder. This was to be Richard's revenge, his kill and he couldn't, wouldn't, leave it to another to even do battle with Firebeard. Ed, a mere-mortal, like all others, wasn't able to kill a demon pirate such as Captain Firebeard, so it had to be someone who'd dealt with the gods to make the kill. Despite knowing this, that didn't stop Richard shooting the man who had been his only true friend during all his years at sea, shooting him for even daring to approach and consider a battle against a man he marked for his own.

The waves splashed ever higher as rain beat down on the deck and the two captains drew their blades, one blade of fire and another of voodoo steel. The thrusting and parrying went on for an endless time. These two skilled sword fighters of the sea were locked in a fierce battle. Both of these men were the only one able to kill the other, locked as they were by a voodoo curse and devil's trade respectively; a mere-mortal couldn't claim the life of these feared sailors, these men dubbed "devils of the sea" by those who'd suffered at their hand.

As the deck lay covered in rain, sea and blood, the surface became very unstable underfoot and as The Silent Reaper rocked Captain Firebeard slipped and fell, and in that instant his heart was struck true. The Walking Dead Man's blade had run him through. "This is for my wife, my dear sweet Marie, and for my parents, the life you took from me." Richard spoke those words as his sword struck hard and true. "When tomorrow's sun rises you will be forgotten," said Richard as he removed his cast blade, and in the moment of his death Firebeard looked in the eye of his killer and said "my soul is free tonight".

Because like Richard many years ago, Firebeard was just another man from another town who had made a deal with the devil, but Richard broke that chain. It was as Firebeard lay fallen and wounded on the deck, in a puddle of his own blood and in his final moments, he looked to his left and he saw the dying face of Richard's first-mate, who was himself just moments from crossing to the other side. The shock was visible on both men's faces, the glance had revealed so much, as the two fallen men lay side by side. Captain Firebeard was John McVeigh, Ed's brother who had cast him aside for the gold that lay in Devil's Mouth all those years ago. Ed was too weak to speak, just seconds from his final breath but the look in his eyes said more than words. Richard was stood with sword still in hand, looking down on both men as his fallen enemy spoke his final words in the direction of his dying brother – "I'm sorry, my brother," he tearfully spoke, his voice shaking with emotion and regret. He carried on while looking into Ed's eyes. "I should have known the gold would cost me all things that were truly valuable, things that cannot be replaced, money truly holds no value when compared to a full heart." As he finished those words, Ed was gone, drawing his final breath, facing his brother with a smile that suggested a forgiveness he could not speak. How brief and how painful this reunion between two brothers was, once so close but driven apart by the lure of gold, now they lay dying side by side at sea; perhaps this was always their fate. Teary and keeping watch on his fallen brother, John McVeigh drew his very last breath, shutting his eyes for the final time.

No sooner had he passed that the rain began fading and the sun to rise, a deafening moan came from the sea beneath them and the clouds did part. Light once again came down from above, this devil of the seas and his darkness had been taken.

Richard and his remaining crew rushed back to Marie's Red Revenge as The Silent Reaper began to be taken down beneath the waves as it broke free from Richard's ship. Reunited in their final moments, John and Ed now lay dead on the deck as The Silent Reaper descended beneath the waves. A new dawn was coming as they faced their forever sunset, with no grave to mark them and no place to remember them, they belong to time and mythology, and together will forever rest under the waves, now existing only in this tale and in legend.

CHAPTER XIII: SAILING FOREVER

The howling winds ceased, the waves calmed and the ocean was once again a vast canvas to travel upon as the light grew stronger with the new day.

As Richard sailed onward without his first-mate, he felt unsteady, although not for the loss of Ed. His heart was now long devoid of any emotion or sentiment within, apart from that of the aching loss of Marie and his parents, the life he could never have back. His unease grew because he felt neither pride nor unburdened by what he'd done – revenge may have removed the man who had caused him such suffering, but he now had no quest and yet his ship must sail on forever over the seas.

Richard had now taken the place of the man for whom he had so much hatred, and no person upon land or sea has the power to free Richard from those chains. He is the new devil of the sea, "The Walking Dead Man", feared by all and a target of revenge for many, just like Firebeard was to him.

Marie is long dead and an angel above, and a devil may never receive an angel's touch, an endless and empty life is all that lay ahead. There will be no reunion in heaven with the woman he loved, nor with his parents, for heaven is a place Richard will never step. Revenge drove him but also ultimately cost him all he ever held dear; he will forever sail the ocean with a heart that is beyond healing and always aching. All who cross his path will meet with a violent end as he seeks to drown the sadness that will always consume him.

This is where this book ends; however, we may never see an end to the story, so be warned and watch out if you see Richard Forsyth sailing your way.